THE FOX'S HICCUPS

NICK BUTTERWORTH

Collins

An Imprint of HarperCollins*Publishers*

The first stars were beginning to
show in the sky as Percy the
park keeper made his way home to his
hut in the park.

He had been working hard all day
and he was tired and hungry. Now he
was looking forward to his supper and
a good rest.

As Percy plodded on he saw his friend
the fox coming up the path
towards him. The fox was on his way
home too.

"Good night," said Percy as they
passed each other.

"Good night, hic-Percy," answered
the fox.

The fox had hiccups.

The fox had been drinking some
fizzy lemonade when a squirrel
told him a funny joke about a parrot,
a worm, and a cricket bat.

The fox exploded with laughter. It was
then that he had learnt that it is not a
good idea to laugh and drink at the same
time. He had had hiccups all afternoon.

"I wonder if hic-Percy knows a good
cure for hic-cups," the fox said to himself.
"I th-hic I'll ask him," he said and with
that he turned and followed after Percy.

When he got back to his hut, Percy remembered that he still had one or two jobs to do. First, he watered some plants.

"I'd better get my washing in too," said Percy. "Then, it's two boiled eggs for me and a pile of toast soldiers."

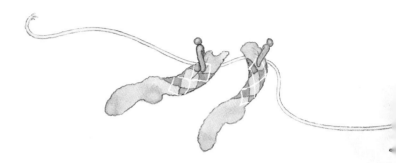

The fox hurried on. He wasn't afraid of the dark. He just liked the light better, that's all. But where was Percy?

He ran round the side of the hut, but instead of finding Percy, he found Percy's washing. Then, with a crash and a tumble which hurt his foot, he found a pile of flower pots.

"Oooowww-hic-ooww!" wailed the fox.

ercy was surprised by the crash.
He stuck his head round the corner.
But when Percy saw what had made the
crash, he quickly pulled it back again.

"It's. . .it's a ghost!" he gasped.

Percy had never met a ghost before. He felt he should introduce himself. But what should he say to a ghost?

Percy listened hard. He could hear the ghost still moaning and thumping about. Suddenly, there was another loud crash, then silence.

Percy was just beginning to wonder if perhaps the ghost had disappeared when there came another sound. A small sound. It was not the sort of sound that Percy expected to hear from a ghost.

"Hic. . .burp."

A smile spread over Percy's face.

Percy poked his head round the corner again. This time, what he saw made him roar with laughter.

"Do you need any help, Mr Ghost?" said Percy, still laughing.

"Yes, please," came a muffled reply from inside the barrel. "Could you possibly turn me the right way up?"

Percy helped the fox back on to his feet.
"You gave me quite a shock," said
Percy.

"I gave myself one," said the fox.
"But it seems to have cured my hiccups!"

NICK BUTTERWORTH

Nick Butterworth was born in North London in 1946 and grew up in a sweet-shop in Essex. He now lives in Suffolk with his wife Annette and their two children, Ben and Amanda.

The inspiration for the Percy's Park books came from Nick's many walks through the local park with the family dog, Jake. *One Snowy Night,* the first story about Percy the park keeper and his animal friends, was published in 1989 and was an instant success. Now stories about Percy and his friends are firm favourites with children everywhere.